POEMS FOR FATHERS

POEMS FOR FATHERS

SELECTED BY
Myra Cohn Livingston

ILLUSTRATED BY
Robert Casilla

Holiday House / New York

Printed in the United States of America
First Edition

LIBRARY OF CONGRESS
Library of Congress Cataloging-in-Publication Data

Poems for fathers / selected by Myra Cohn Livingston; illustrated by
Robert Casilla.
p. cm.
Summary: Eighteen poems by English and American authors celebrate
fathers—sometimes humorously, sometimes poignantly.
ISBN 0-8234-0729-2
1. Fathers—Juvenile poetry.   2. Children's poetry, American.
3. Children's poetry, English.   [1. Fathers—Poetry.   2. American
poetry—Collections.   3. English poetry—Collections.]
I. Livingston, Myra Cohn.   II. Casilla, Robert, ill.
PS595.F39P64 1989
811′.008′0352043—dc19   88-17010   CIP   AC

ISBN 0-8234-0729-2

CONTENTS

I Like It When

I like it sometimes when we meet
in deepest downtown,
all the way down on Fifth Street
for haircuts. They drape us in gowns.

I like it when we're deep inside the mirror
together, the scissors clicking away.
The hair beneath your swivel chair
is shiny black or milky gray.

I like it sometimes when they shave our chins,
you with a razor and me not.
The lather's cold against our skins,
the air around us August hot.

Why does the barber say your cut becomes you?
Becoming you is hard to do.

RICHARD MARGOLIS

Snowstorm

Only my dad was brave enough
To drive through snowstorms.
Bundled up, I sat by his side
Watching the wipers
Push away heavy globs of snow.
Our car zigzagged
Across the icy road
Like a skater
Trying to make the hill,
While all around
Other cars were stopped and stuck;
Their drivers
Standing outside, blowing streams of smoke,
Eyed us as we reached the top.

KAREN B. WINNICK

Daddy

only know I loved you
     Daddy
watched you
hoping someday
     maybe
me and you'd
do things real
     crazy
always hoped
you'd call me
     baby

didn't see
that things were
     shabby
couldn't tell
things went so
     badly
never knew
you were
     unhappy
only knew I loved you
     Daddy

MYRA COHN LIVINGSTON

Age Four and My Father

Once upon a long ago
he invited me to take his hand
and after supper walk along
the silver summer sand.
I'd never known the dark before
or seen the welcome of a star
until we went beyond our door
and wandered, silent, very far
into a world of moon and night
our love a lantern, briefly bright.

JULIA CUNNINGHAM

Different Dads

Training horses, riding fire trucks—
Some dads do that. Other dads
Mostly sit and scribble figures
On computers, or ruled pads.

Fixing bikes, some fathers falter
Even though for years they've tried.
When they're done, your chain will dangle
Every time you start to ride.

That's why when my bike has problems
I ask Mom. Poor helpless Dad
Can't twist wrenches or ply pliers—
Otherwise, he's not half bad.

Truth is, he's a whiz at adding.
Once when I didn't dig my math
He explained it, writing numbers
With the soapsuds of my bath.

Then there was the time my bedroom
Had a visitor—a bat—
And what superhero trapped it
Gently in my baseball hat?

Father. Could you find one better?
Maybe. But you'd travel far.
Any fathers have their uses.
Doesn't matter who they are.

X.J. KENNEDY

Christmas Wish

Daddy, you are gone away.
You are a long time gone.
Still, I hear your gravel voice
speak—something like a song.

Everyone hugs everyone
around the twinkling tree.
Daddy, *now* I miss you most.
I wish you could hug me.

TONY JOHNSTON

12

Daddy's Gone

Tonight their voices screeched
And the screen door banged;
Daddy packed his bags,
Now he's gone.
The sky sags, hot and crooked,
And the moon hangs wrong,
        I hear a shrill and crazy
        Crickets' song.

Daddy taught me
If we listened close and still,
We'd hear bright tiny words
The crickets speak.
We listened—
His whiskers brushed my cheek.
        Tonight those words rise
        In a rasping shriek.

Nothing moves,
Yet the porch light's yellow glare
Cannot hold back
The crickets' awful song.
Thick and blackly,
On and on and on
        The crickets keep repeating,
        "Daddy's gone."

DEBORAH CHANDRA

Daddy Fell into the Pond

Everyone grumbled. The sky was grey.
We had nothing to do and nothing to say.
We were nearing the end of a dismal day,
And their seemed to be nothing beyond,
                    THEN
        Daddy fell into the pond!

And everyone's face grew merry and bright,
And Timothy danced for sheer delight.
"Give me the camera, quick, oh quick!
He's crawling out of the duckweed.!"   *Click!*

Then the gardener suddenly slapped his knee,
And doubled up, shaking silently,
And the ducks all quacked as if they were daft
And it sounded as if the old drake laughed.

Oh, there wasn't a thing that didn't respond
                    WHEN
        Daddy fell into the pond!

ALFRED NOYES

15

Father William

"You are old, Father William," the young man said
    "And your hair has become very white;
And yet you incessantly stand on your head—
    Do you think, at your age, it is right?"

"In my youth," Father William replied to his son,
    "I feared it might injure the brain;
But, now that I'm perfectly sure I have none,
    Why, I do it again and again."

"You are old," said the youth, "as I mentioned before,
　　　And have grown most uncommonly fat;
Yet you turned a back-somersault in at the door—
　　　Pray, what is the reason of that?"

"In my youth," said the sage, as he shook his grey locks,
　　　"I kept all my limbs very supple
By the use of this ointment—one shilling the box—
　　　Allow me to sell you a couple?"

"You are old," said the youth, "and your jaws are too weak
    For anything tougher than suet;
Yet you finished the goose, with the bones and the beak—
    Pray, how did you manage to do it?"

"In my youth," said his father, "I took to the law,
    And argued each case with my wife;
And the muscular strength which it gave to my jaw
    Has lasted the rest of my life."

"You are old," said the youth, "one would hardly suppose
    That your eye was as steady as ever;
Yet you balanced an eel on the end of your nose—
    What made you so awfully clever?"

"I have answered three questions, and that is enough,"
    Said his father. "Don't give yourself airs!
Do you think I can listen all day to such stuff?
    Be off, or I'll kick you downstairs!"

LEWIS CARROLL

Papa Is a Bear

Papa is a morning bear—
Showers, pats his grizzly hair,
Throws his clothes on, scares the cat,
Shuffles down to breakfast. That
Closet is his hiding place,
BOO!, hugs Mama, rubs my face
With his whiskers, eats his grits,
Growls again before he sits
In his den to read the news,
Winks at me, unties his shoes;
Papa's ready for a snooze.

J. PATRICK LEWIS

20

Counting Sleep

1
2
My daddy, who
3
4
stands at the door,
5
6
he can fix
7
8
any late
9
10
monsters, when

10
9
they come to dine.
8
7
It is heaven
6
5
to be alive
4
3
and know that he
2
1
fears none!

LUCILLE CLIFTON

21

Mummy Slept Late and
Daddy Fixed Breakfast

Daddy fixed the breakfast.
He made us each a waffle.
It looked like gravel pudding.
It tasted something awful.

"Ha, ha," he said, "I'll try again.
This time I'll get it right."
But what *I* got was in between
Bituminous and anthracite.

"A little too well done? Oh well,
I'll have to start all over."
That time what landed on my plate
Looked like a manhole cover.

I tried to cut it with a fork:
The fork gave off a spark.
I tried a knife and twisted it
Into a question mark.

I tried it with a hacksaw.
I tried it with a torch.
It didn't even make a dent.
It didn't even scorch.

The next time Dad gets breakfast
When Mommy's sleeping late,
I think I'll skip the waffles.
I'd sooner eat the plate!

JOHN CIARDI

My Father's Words

"Our only little girl,
 and we're pretty proud of her."

My father's words
as we meet his friends
outside the movie—

Proud of me?

I know
my parents love me,
but "proud"
I've never heard—
And he tells his friends
it's so!

The word
leaps into me
and I become
one big exclamation point
shooting up, up!
all the way home.

CLAUDIA LEWIS

My José

When he sees friends come home with me
he always says hello,
and if they're new friends
I'm supposed to tell their names and his name.
The problem is I don't know what to call him.

Stepfather is strange.

He's not my dad.

Mister is an uptight word.

I try to get outdoors to play
before he notices,
but if I can't I finally just say,

Hey guys, this is my José.

MARTHA ROBINSON

Saturday Fielding Practice

I'll never win a prize
for shagging flies.

My father hits them out
to me and Sis.

She catches most of them.
I often miss.

"That's OK, John," Dad says,
"her legs are long.

Give it a year or two.
You'll be as strong."

Baseball is fun, I guess,
but I keep wishing

that next week Saturday
Dad takes us fishing.

LILLIAN MORRISON

Father and I in the Woods

"Son,"
  My father used to say,
"Don't run."

"Walk,"
  My father used to say,
"Don't talk."

"Words,"
  My father used to say,
"Scare birds."

So be:
  It's sky and brook and bird
  And tree.

DAVID MCCORD

Father's Magic

Hundreds of starlings
landed on my trees.
"Come, look," my father said.
He clapped his hands,
once, twice,
and all the starlings
flew away.

EMANUEL DI PASQUALE

Carving Pumpkins with My Father

Being small, I always choose
the largest I can find,
thump the yellow rind
like a melon,
then watch him carry it home.

First, he slices off the top.
We scoop out strings of seeds
and make the ears, small hoops of light,
the slanting eyes. Then I draw the nose:
a jagged O.
But with great care we carve
the ragged grimace
tooth by tooth,
two dark bent heads grinning
pumpkin-like ourselves,
taking turns
till the last tooth is cut.

Then we stand at the window
and watch our street
aflicker with smiles
till the first stars arise
till the last lights blow out.

LIZ ROSENBERG

ACKNOWLEDGMENTS

Grateful acknowledgment is made to the following poets, whose work was especially commissioned for this book:

Deborah Chandra for "Daddy's Gone." Copyright © 1989 by Deborah Chandra.

Lucille Clifton for "Counting Sleep." Copyright © 1989 by Lucille Clifton.

Julia Cunningham for "Age Four and My Father." Copyright © 1989 by Julia Cunningham.

Emanuel di Pasquale for "Father's Magic." Copyright © 1989 by Emanuel di Pasquale.

Tony Johnston for "Christmas Wish." Copyright © 1989 by Tony Johnston.

X.J. Kennedy for "Different Dads." Copyright © 1989 by X.J. Kennedy.

Claudia Lewis for "My Father's Words." Copyright © 1989 by Claudia Lewis.

J. Patrick Lewis for "Papa Is a Bear." Copyright © 1989 by J. Patrick Lewis.

Richard Margolis for "I Like It When." Copyright © 1989 by Richard Margolis.

Lillian Morrison for "Saturday Fielding Practice." Copyright © 1989 by Lillian Morrison.

Martha Robinson for "My José." Copyright © 1989 by Martha Robinson.

Liz Rosenberg for "Carving Pumpkins with my Father." Copyright © 1989 by Liz Rosenberg.

Karen B. Winnick for "Snowstorm." Copyright © 1989 by Karen B. Winnick.

Grateful acknowledgment is also made for the following reprints:

Atheneum Publishers for "Daddy" (published as "Leroy") from *No Way of Knowing: Dallas Poems* by Myra Cohn Livingston. Copyright © 1980 by Myra Cohn Livingston. (A Margaret K. McElderry Book). Reprinted with the permission of Atheneum Publishers, Inc.

Harper & Row, Publishers, Inc. for "Mummy Slept Late and Daddy Fixed Breakfast" from *You Read to Me and I'll Read to You* by John Ciardi. Copyright © 1962 by John Ciardi. Reprinted by permission of Harper & Row, Publishers, Inc.

Little, Brown and Company for "Father and I in the Woods" by David McCord from *One at a Time*. Copyright © 1974 by David McCord. Reprinted by permission of Little, Brown and Company.

Sheed & Ward for "Daddy Fell into the Pond" by Alfred Noyes from *Daddy Fell into the Pond and Other Poems*. Copyright © 1952 by Alfred Noyes. Used with permission of Sheed & Ward, 115 E. Armour Blvd., Kansas City, MO.